f i n

But I never promised anything
about my little sister...

And when she'd finished telling me off she made me promise cross-my-heart, that I would never – ever – swap my dad for anything ever ever again.

And I promised.

So I won't.

When we got home my mother said things like, "Just look at the state of him!" and she made him go and have a bath and she put all his clothes into the washing.

While dad was in the bath, my mother told me off.

Last week my little sister told everyone at school that I was adopted. The week before she told everyone at school that I was a space alien pretending to be me.

There was a little rabbit hutch there,
and next to the rabbit hutch was a little
run with chicken wire all around it.
My dad sat on the grass, in the chicken wire run,
reading his newspaper and eating a carrot.
He looked a bit lonely, and he had grass all
over his trousers.

They took the rabbit away from us and fussed over it, and gave it some lettuce.

Patti took my hand

Thank you for bringing Galveston back,

she said.

"We missed it".

We walked into the back garden.

While we walked, Galveston the Rabbit sat in my arms and made its nose go woffly. My sister tried to make her nose go as woffly as Galveston's but she couldn't do it.

I gave him the gorilla mask. He gave me Galveston
and a map he drew of how to get to Patti's house.

I'd never walked so far in my whole life.

Blinky came down the big stairs.
He looked very pleased to see the
gorilla mask.

"Are you bringing
it back?" he asked.

"Yes we are,"
I told him.

The butler came out.

Blinky had a very big house.
We went up to the front and rang the bell.

So we went to Nathan's house.
He only lives over the road.
I knocked on the door.

Nathan's mother came out.

Is Nathan here?

I asked.

"Where did you get those goldfish," she asked me.

They were a present to Nathan from his Aunt Violet."

"I swapped them," I said. "And now I have to swap them back again."

My mother looked at me sharply.

Young man, she said.

Is this true?

She only calls me Young Man if she's very, very mad.

Yes, I said.

"Right", said my mother, and she picked up the bowl of goldfish and handed it to me. "You can take these goldfish over to Nathan this minute, and don't you come back without your father."

"I told you so," said my little sister.

"And you can go with him," said my mother. "Fancy allowing your brother to swap your father for two goldfish and a bowl. The very idea."

When my mother came home I said, "Mom, can we buy some goldfish food?"

I thought for a bit.

Some people have great ideas maybe once or twice in their life, and then they discover electricity or fire or outer space or something.
I mean, the kind of brilliant ideas that change the whole world.

Some people never have them at all.

We went up to my bedroom.
My little sister tagged along.
I showed Nathan my old transformer
robots, and my baseball cards, and my books.
I showed him my old punching bag and my
penny whistle that Mommy said made her
head ache when I blew it. I showed him
my old spaceship that didn't float in the
bath any more, and the puppet with the
tangled strings, and I even showed him
Clownie, my clown that I sleep with.

One day my mom went out and left me at home
with just my little sister and my dad.

My dad sat in front of the
television, reading his newspaper.
My dad doesn't pay much attention
to anything, when he's reading his
newspaper.

Wanted: One halibut, must be in good working order, own fins, no skate please.

Will swap two infants, one called Yolanda, one called Liam, both house trained, except Liam.

Offers to Mr. David Tench McKean Esq. c/o The Publisher.

ThE DAY i swapped my DAD for TWO goldfisH

neilGaiman & dave McKean

Lost: One book. If found please return to Hayley Campbell (although she may be too big for it)

or Maddy Gaiman (although it may be too big for her).

No fish, please.

SCHOLASTIC INC.

New York Toronto London Auckland Sydney
Mexico City New Delhi Hong Kong

RIVER

ISBN 0-590-63189-6

Copyright © 1997 by Neil Gaiman and Dave McKean. All rights reserved.
Published by Scholastic Inc., 555 Broadway, New York, NY 10012,
by arrangement with White Wolf Publishing.
SCHOLASTIC and associated logos are trademarks and/or registered
trademarks of Scholastic Inc.

12 11 10 9 8 7 6 5 4 3 2 1   9/9 0 1 2 3 4/0

Printed in the U.S.A.   14

First Scholastic paperback printing, February 1999

Book design by Dave McKean @ Hourglass